by Leigh Anne Florence

Illustrations by Paul Brett Johnson

International Standard Book Number 978-0-9844645-0-0
Library of Congress Card Catalog Number 2010924915

Cover design and Illustrations by Paul Brett Johnson
Book layout by 2 Paws Up

Manufactured in the United States of America

All book order correspondence should be addressed to:

HotDiggetyDog Press
P.O. 747
Shepherdsville, KY 40165

502-376-5966
leighanne@thewoodybooks.com
www.thewoodybooks.com

Dedication

This book is dedicated to our farmers, forest rangers, park rangers, and those who love the great outdoors.

Thank you for protecting and preserving our American wilderness for our future generations.

Foreward
by Leigh Anne Florence

In early 2009, Woody and I began working on our sixth serial story for the Kentucky Press Association. From the very beginning we imagined a good ol' fashioned camping trip complete with fishing, campfires, s'mores, and predicaments. Since we've done our fair share of camping, we had a good concept of the material, yet we quickly realized our information was rather limited. We needed some expert advice. Obviously my husband Ron was a wealth of information. Ron is the ultimate Boy Scout. He can build a fire, build a fort, and catch, clean, and cook his supper. Ron can survive in any situation with ease. (That's obvious since he lives with a wife, seven dogs, one cat, and one bathroom!) We also spent a great deal of time in conversation with our veterinarian, Dr. Chris Albert Carnes. Dr. Albert, as her patients call her, explained the routines and habitats of different animals, pointed out various trees and bushes, shared her experiences with creek stomping and covered what ailments animals could suffer from while outside. Ron and Dr. Albert provided vital information that I used heavily while writing, but I couldn't write this story without the help of our dear friends in Mayfield, KY, Greg and Michele Douglas. If anyone knew about enjoying and surviving the outdoors, it was Greg and Michele.

Greg and I grew up in the same community, attended the same school and church, and shared a love for whacky humor. Greg received a Bachelor's Degree in Agriculture and a Master's Degree in Agronomy (the science and technology of using plants for food, fuel, feed, and fiber). Greg was a successful farmer who loved to fish and hunt. He loved the land and knew how to treat the earth with respect. When I told Greg our next story was going to focus on the outdoors, he began spouting off a list of things I must cover. It became a regular routine for Greg to call me several days a week. He would always call at noon while he was taking his lunch break from farming. Greg would say, "I've thought of something you have to use in the story. Get a pen and write this down." Then he would say, "Where's my royalty check?" My reply was always the same – "You haven't gotten that yet? I intend to contact the Postal Service and find out what's taking them so long in delivering your money!" He would laugh in the heartiest, most contagious laugh I had ever heard. I was so excited for Greg to see this finished product. Sadly, it didn't happen that way. Greg passed away on December 19, 2009 – just 17 days after he turned 44 as a result of a heart defect. He left behind his beautiful and strong wife, Michele, and twin daughters, Kassey and Callie.

Through Greg, I learned so many things about our great land. I also learned some very important outdoor survival skills – especially during those phone conversations he and I shared. In the days and weeks following Greg's death, I have realized that Michele is such a strong survivor too. Michele, a National Board Certified English teacher in Graves County, Kentucky plans to continue farming during her summer breaks. By doing so, her daughters can develop an even deeper love and appreciation for our great earth.

I wish Greg could have seen this book *Dog Gone Wild*. The important part however is that his knowledge and passion for our great land will be shared with every reader for years and years to come. That will be just one of the many legacies Greg Douglas will leave to Michele, his daughters Kassey and Callie, his family, and all of us who loved him so dearly.

Words from Woody

Mom, Dad, Chloe, Frannie, and Wally – Thanks for giving me a great home and showing me what it really means to be a survivor!

Paul Brett Johnson – We are thrilled to have such a creative and fun Kentucky illustrator on our team! Your book *On Top of Spaghetti* is our favorite!

The WOODY TEAM – Lynne, Sue, Nathan, and Shaun - Your hard work behind the scenes makes our job a piece of cake!

Our friends at the Kentucky Press Association and the Lexington Herald-Leader – David, Kriss, Steve, Rusty, and Kevin – We do the fun part and you do all the rest! Thanks for making us shine in the newspapers each week!

Scott and Kat – Thanks for being our voice! It's music to our ears!

Diane – The yummy treats in the *Emergency Roadside Assistance Bag* you prepare for us make traveling – and being stuck on the side of the road – much more enjoyable!

Our veterinarians – Dr. Chris Albert Carnes, Dr. James Cecil, and all the staff at Mount Washington Animal Clinic; Dr. Scott Campbell, Dr. Chris Reeder, and all the staff at Metropolitan Veterinary Services – Thanks for keeping us healthy all year long! By the way, Dr. Cecil, thanks for nominating me for the 2009 Kentucky Veterinary Medical Association Hall of Fame. That is a huge honor!

Louisville Gas & Electric/Kentucky Utilities – E.ON U.S. – especially Cliff Feltham, Chris Hermann, and Chip Keeling as well as the Kentucky Secretary of State - Thank you for sponsoring this program.

The Kentucky newspapers and all the schools who participated in the ***Dog Gone Wild*** series - Thanks for being faithful readers!

And finally, to you – our friends - for reading our books, attending our events, sending us kind letters and emails, and giving us sweet hugs and kisses on the road! Our family loves and appreciates each of you! Keep that spirit of survival and ***Work and Dream like a BIG DOG***!

Chapter 1

My big break! My chance to shine! My opportunity to show my family that I'm a warrior, a champion, a real sportsman, uh, sports-dog! I'm sorry, I should introduce myself. I'm Mr. Dogwood, but my friends and family call me Woody. (Sometimes I'll hear "Dogwood" if I've made a knucklehead decision or if my parents are trying to get my attention.) Anyway, I'm a black and tan miniature wiener dog who lives in the great state where I was born – Kentucky, making me "Woody, The Kentucky Wiener." I'm just like any other wiener dog. I like mealtime, chasing cats, and digging - only I have a job. That's right – a regular set the alarm, carry my briefcase, get a paycheck job! My big sister Chloe (a redheaded miniature wiener dog), my human parents (Mom and Dad) and I travel around in The *Woody Bus* talking to kids and adults about being their best. We call it *Woody's Five Ways to Be Successful.* Mom, Dad, Chloe, and I hope we help others, all the while reminding ourselves, that with hard work, a positive attitude, respect for others and ourselves, we can accomplish great things. Mom and Dad tell Chloe and me every day that we can achieve all our goals and dreams. "Work and dream like a big dog, Woody!" Dad once told me. "It doesn't matter that you're little, just think big. That, plus a winning attitude and hard work will take you places!" That was the best advice I'd heard. In

PUPCORN

fact, it's become my motto! Now, Mom, Dad, Chloe, and I travel all around and share that message with others. How great is that!

Where was I? Oh, my big break. It started when my family was gathered around our TV watching our favorite show – a competition about surviving outdoors. During the course of the show, people live outdoors, participate in different challenges, and try to survive. The person who can stay in the game the longest by finding their own food, braving the elements, and staying tough is declared the winner. The winner gets to brag to everyone how he or she survived – and goes away with a great big money prize! Anyway, Mom, Dad, Chloe, and I were glued to the television watching as the competitors had to hike 12 miles up a mountain and use a grapevine to swing across a river that was filled with crocodiles before they were safe. I made the comment that it seemed like a simple task.

"Simple?" Chloe asked, "It doesn't look simple to me. Besides Woody, you get tired on our two mile walk every morning. Do you really think you could hike 12 miles and fend off crocodiles?"

"Sure I could. If faced with the challenge, I would prevail every time!" I responded, puffing my chest out a bit. I thought the conversation was closed until Dad said, "Hey, let's put you to the test! How about the four of us take an old fashioned camping trip?"

"TerRUFFic idea!" I barked! "Can we compete like they do on the show?"

"Sure, your Mom and I will come up with challenges and you and Chloe can compete."

Secretly I smiled. Piece of cake! My sister was the smartest and prettiest girl I knew, but I was the guy, the man, the brute! I could hear it now, "Game over, Woody won!" Mom must have read my thoughts because she said, "Remember, Woody, it's a friendly competition and your sister is tougher than you think!"

"Yes Ma'am," I replied. "Since it is a competition, what's the grand prize?" I asked.

Dad thought for a minute and said, "Since the winner of the show receives money, the winner of our family will receive money too – a new, crisp $50.00 bill!"

I'd been wanting a new bowling game for my *Woof*. Fifty dollars would do the trick! I was getting ready to browse the Internet to find the game I was going to buy when Dad said, "Here's your first challenge: You and Chloe must each pack your own backpack of things you will need for the camping trip. You can only take one bag so make sure you pack smart – taking only things that will be useful. Get your bag packed because we will leave as soon as the sun comes up in the morning!"

"In the morning? At sun up? That's early!" I replied. For some reason, Mom, Dad, and Chloe laughed. I must have missed the joke but unfortunately, I didn't have time to ask what was funny. I had to get focused. I had a competition to win and my first challenge was getting my backpack ready. And for the life of me, I couldn't remember where Mom kept the blankets.

Chapter 2

Who knew packing a backpack could be so challenging?

At sunrise, our family crawled in our trusty Woody Bus. Though sleepy, I was excited for our adventure. I knew with the challenges of our camping week that I needed my strength. "Dad, before we leave town, can we run through the drive-through? I've a hankering for a bacon sandwich."

"Woody, we haven't left the driveway! Besides,we won't be eating fast food or stopping at restaurants. We'll be having picnics with the food we packed."

I loved picnics, but it was hard telling my tummy to wait! Thankfully, I'd packed some snacks, but I needed to save those for later. Needing to occupy my mind, I made a suggestion. "Hey Chloe, let's play *I Spy*!" For the next hour, we spied water towers, stop signs, cornfields, and even a brand new baby foal. When we were tired from our detective work, Chloe said, "Let's play the *Alphabet Game*. We'll use things we packed for our trip."

"Super!" Mom praised. "I'll start! A – atlas."

"B, batteries" Dad continued.

"C, compass" Chloe said. She always took the letter C since her name began with that letter. "Your turn Woody."

"D – D – D..." "Uh, I'll take the next letter."

TRAIL

"D – drinking water," Mom helped.

"E - electric blanket," I exclaimed! Once I said 'electric blanket,' Chloe giggled, Mom turned around, and Dad hit the brakes and pulled over to the side of the road. Everyone stared at me. From the looks on their faces, I could tell what they were thinking. They were jealous! They couldn't believe they hadn't thought about bringing an electric blanket. I was plenty of things, but I wasn't selfish. It was a big blanket and there was room for all four of us. I would share.

"Woody," Dad said, "where will you plug in the electric blanket?"

"Plug in?" I repeated.

"Yes, Woody," Dad continued. "what do you plan on plugging the blanket into so it will get warm?"

My heart skipped a beat. I hadn't thought about needing electricity. Sure, there were times during a storm when the power went out, but that was only for a brief time. It was no easy task cramming the blanket and the cord into my backpack.

Oh no, it just hit me! No electricity meant no television, no video games, no computer, no updating my *DogFace* page, no microwave, no refrigerator, no…

"Woody," Mom interrupted, "what else did you pack?"

There was no getting around it. I had to answer. I swallowed hard and began listing the contents of my bag. "An electric blanket, my swimming trunks, my favorite Scooby Doo art set, my *WOOF*, some microwave popcorn, and a few cherry pupscicles. Oh, I almost forgot. I brought my harmonica too."

"PUPSCICLES?" Mom screamed, "IN YOUR BACKPACK?" Mom didn't wait for an answer. She found my backpack and began emptying it. My trunks were sticky from the melting treats. Mom was getting ready to throw the pupscicles out when I said, "Can't we eat them?" Mom and Dad had funny looks on their face. I offered a pupscicle to Chloe, but she was shaking too hard, trying to contain her laughter.

Packing our backpack was our first challenge and it looked like I had failed. How could I recover? "Dad, you may think what I have in my backpack is silly, but we don't know what Chloe packed." I secretly hoped Chloe had a hair dryer or computer in her bag. My sister opened her backpack and pulled out each item. Chloe's bag contained a compass, a raincoat, a first aid kit, flashlight, sleeping bag, jerky, trail mix, a radio, a cell phone, and a small book titled *Camping for Canines – and People Too*. I was getting ready to make a comment about the radio and cell phone when Chloe explained the radio was a battery operated weather radio and the cell phone was charged to use only in the case of an emergency.

Mom and Dad complimented Chloe for her smart choices. Dad explained that surviving in any situation depended on making intelligent choices and being prepared. I was curious how Chloe chose those items so I asked. "Well," Chloe explained, "I remembered reading a newspaper article once about camping. I knew the sleeping bag and rain coat would keep me warm; the flashlight, weather radio, and first aid kit would keep me safe; and the jerky and trail mix would keep me fed – and it wouldn't spoil." Chloe had based her choices on her most basic needs – like being safe and warm. It was obvious Chloe had won our first challenge. Thankfully, my sister wasn't selfish. I had a feeling I would be borrowing things from her pack in the near future.

Chapter 3

When our family travels, Dad drives, Mom rides shotgun, and Chloe and I sit in the backseat playing games, singing songs, and even watching DVDs from time to time. I never know where we are, where we are going, and how long it will take to get there, so "Are we there yet?" is my standard question. Usually, Dad answers, "Not yet, Woody. It's going to be another hour or so, just sit tight." This time, Dad surprised me. "Woody, I thought you'd never ask. Your next challenge is to study the map and navigate our course," Dad explained as Mom handed both Chloe and me a map. There was one problem. How could I navigate when I didn't know what the word meant? Mom explained that *navigate* meant to direct, to guide, or to plot the course of the trip. Dad wanted Chloe and me to look at the map and direct him to our destination.

Destination? That was my second problem. Where were we going?

"We're going to the *Daniel Boone Campground,*" Dad informed.

"Daniel Boone? If I'd known I would have brought my coonskin cap!"

I looked at Chloe. She was studying the colorful map. I

knew this was a challenge, but I needed help. "Chloe, can you help me get started?"

"Sure Woody. The first thing you should do is turn your map around. It's upside down." No wonder I was confused! Ah, that was better!

"Chloe, how about another clue?"

"I'd love to help, Woody, but I'm confused too." Chloe pulled out her compass. It showed we were traveling east.

"The sun also tells us we are traveling east," Mom said. "The sun comes up every morning in the east. If the sun comes up in the east, and we're driving into the sun, we must be traveling east."

Moms are so smart! "But how can I find east on the map?" I asked. Mom told me to look at the legend. First *navigate,* now *legend.* I sure wish I'd packed a dictionary.

Seeing my confusion, Mom continued. "The legend is the chart on the map that explains the symbols." I found the chart. I saw N at the top, S at the bottom, E on the right side, and W on the left side. "E for east! We are traveling to the right side of the map!" I said, as my paw traveled toward the right side of the paper. "But where?"

As I was asking my questions, Chloe said, "Look! I found the *Daniel Boone Campground*!" I asked Chloe to show me. She pointed to the right corner of the map. "Woody, do you see the green trees and the little green symbol that looks like a tent?" I squinted at the tiny drawing and saw what looked like woods. In little letters, I saw the words "Daniel Boone Campground."

"I see it too! And look – we're close. Slow down, Dad! We're only about three inches away!"

Everyone laughed! It was clear I knew nothing about maps so I swallowed my pride and asked for help. "Dad, I know navigating is a challenge between Chloe and me, but just this once, can Chloe and I work together?" I was expecting Dad to tell me to keep trying, so I was surprised at his answer.

"Great idea, Woody. A rule in surviving is working together to accomplish a task. So yes, this time, instead of competing with Chloe, the two of you can work together."

"Wow! I thought you were going to tell me not to give up!" Dad explained I wasn't giving up; I was just changing my game plan.

With the help of the legend, Chloe and I discovered that the large, colored lines were major highways, the broken lines were little roads, the little blue lines were rivers, and the numbers were the highway numbers.

"Woody," Chloe said, "why don't you look out the window to see if you see any road signs that will give us clues as to what highway we are on?"

"Sure!" I said. "Hey! I just saw a sign that looked like a reindeer walking across the road. How silly! A reindeer should know this is a bad place to cross the road!" Dad explained the sign wasn't for the deer, but so drivers would know to slow down because there were deer in the area. "Ah! That makes sense!" Right after the deer sign, I saw US HWY 80. "Chloe, we are on United States Highway 80!" The moment I said "80," Chloe said, "I found it! I found it!" We now knew where we were, where we were going, and following the colored line we now knew how to get there. But wait, this tiny little road looked like it could be a shortcut…

Chapter 4

What should have been a two-hour trip took four hours! The path Chloe and I chose looked like a shortcut on the map. We didn't take into consideration that the shortcut was a one-lane gravel road that had a speed limit of 35 miles an hour!!! I was getting restless! "Dad, we have been on this road for an hour and haven't seen one single person – much less a police officer! Can't we drive faster – say like 50 miles an hour?"

"Dogwood, the speed limit is 35 miles an hour. That's the law. It's a law and a rule that we will follow whether anybody is looking or not. Besides, the 35 mile speed limit is for our safety."

"Yes sir. I'm sorry. I guess shortcuts don't always mean faster!" Dad agreed and told me to relax and enjoy the scenery. While we looked at the trees, the streams, and the occasional houses we passed, I entertained the family by playing my harmonica. We tried to play *Name that Tune*, but I kept stumping my family! They couldn't name one single tune!

Finally, after four hours, three games of *I Spy,* and at least fifty questions of *"Are we there yet?"* we finally arrived at the *Daniel Boone Campground!* Everything about it was gorgeous! While Dad paid our camping fee and talked with the park

ranger, Mom, Chloe, and I took the time to stretch. I looked at Chloe. She looked serious. "What's wrong?" I asked.

"Nothing, Woody, I am just soaking it all in – the sight of all the green trees around us, the smell of the honeysuckle, the cool way the grass feels under my paws and the warm sun on my ears! Don't you feel it too?"

I stopped and closed my eyes. "Yes, I feel it too!" Something occurred to me. I had spent so much time indoors playing my *WOOF* game that it had been a while since I had played outside. I'd been missing out on some really great sights, sounds, and smells, right outside my own front door. Closing my eyes like Chloe, I was imagining that I was a great frontiersman like Daniel Boone blazing a trail or Davy Crockett fighting off a bear! I was adjusting my imaginary coon-skin cap when Dad arrived and announced we were all set.

"Where should we pitch our tent?" Chloe barked.

"*PITCH* our tent? Chloe, are you crazy? If we throw away our tent, where we will sleep?"

Looking at Chloe, I saw her shaking her head and giggling.

"Really, Woody," Chloe said, "if you're going to be a survivor, you should at least know camping lingo. *Pitching* a tent doesn't mean we are throwing it away, it means we're assembling our tent, or setting it up."

I thought about playing it cool and saying, "I knew that. I was checking to see if you did," but Chloe knew better. Besides, she was right – I did need to know the lingo. Mom was always saying that having a hefty vocabulary was necessary in being successful. "Woody, if you're familiar with plenty of words, you can communicate with people better, understand others more clearly, read a variety of books, learn about various subjects, and survive in any situation."

Once again, Mom was right. I didn't know that my vocabulary – or lack of – would play a role in camping. I was wrong. My limited terminology had just made it difficult to communicate. I was learning that a good rule of survival was being able to communicate with others – and a good vocabulary was key. I made a note to self. I was going to find my dictionary and get to know Mr. Webster as soon as we returned home.

As I was pondering my resolution, Chloe barked. "It says in my camping book that choosing a spot is important. We need to make sure that we are on high, level ground. That way, if it rains the rain won't slide down on us."

"What else does it say?" I asked.

"Well," Chloe continued, "we need to be close enough to a stream so we can have easy access to water. We need to have trees around us that will provide us shade and limbs to hang our items on, but we have to look out for dead branches. We wouldn't want to take a chance on them falling on us. One more thing - which way should our tent face?"

This was a question I could answer. "How about east? That way, the sun will wake us up every morning!" Taking all those things into consideration, we finally found a large piece of ground that we all agreed on! As Dad pulled the tent out of the box, Chloe and I couldn't believe the name of our tent…

Chapter 5

T*he Dependable Pup Tent*! If there were the perfect name for our camping home, it was a pup tent! "Woody," Dad explained, a pup tent refers to a shelter that doesn't have floors or windows. It's also a tent we have to assemble, so let's read the directions."

"Directions?" I barked! "We're smart. We don't need directions."

"Woody, this is our home for the next several days. I think we should read the directions and get it right. A rule in surviving is taking the time to do it right the first time." Mom was always talking about the importance of reading and following directions. "Besides," Dad continued, "I would hate for the tent to collapse while we were trying to sleep."

Thanks to directions and teamwork, we had our home. "Let's go fishing," I suggested, grabbing my pole.

"Not yet, son," Dad answered. "We have to gather wood and kindling for a fire later."

"With the trees around us, that shouldn't take long! Can I borrow your knife, Dad?"

"We can't cut off branches of a perfectly good tree. It could destroy the tree." Dad explained. "We also want to find wood away from the campsite so we won't use all that's here. We

need to respect the land and not use all its resources." I hadn't realized that.

"Anyway, Woody, we all remember what happened the last time you borrowed a knife," Chloe said, reminding me of the silly mistake that meant a trip to the vet last month.

"Dad," I asked, "may Chloe and I walk down the hill and find firewood?"

"Sure, but don't get out of sight and stay together. Remember," Dad instructed, "be respectful. Don't bother any rocks, animals or trees. This is their natural habitat and we have to value that."

Chloe and I promised to obey. As we went in search of firewood, we sang, "*Do your ears hang low, do they wobble to and fro? Can you…* Chloe, why have you stopped singing? The part where we tie our ears in a knot is my favorite part!"

"Woo-dy," Chloe whispered, "Don't move. There's a snake in front of us."

I saw it! My heart began pounding out of my chest. I didn't want Chloe to know how scared I was! I was the brother, the protector. Even though I was scared, I was determined to play it cool. "Don't worry, Chloe. I'll protect you." I said, sounding cool as a cucumber.

"Thanks Woody. I read in my camping book that snakes are more scared of people than we are than them. Besides, I can tell by looking at it that it's not venomous. It is all one color and it has a spoon shaped head, not a flat head. It shouldn't bother us, but I still have the willies! Let's quietly leave."

That was the best idea I'd heard. To be honest, it didn't matter to me if it was venomous or not. And how did the book know the snake was more afraid than we were? Did the author interview snakes? I hoped the snake didn't know where our tent was pitched! Chloe and I left. Walking back to the tent, we found enough dead branches lying on the ground for kindling and were back at the camp within a short time.

"Mom! Dad!" I barked when we arrived at the tent, "You're never going to believe it. Chloe and I saw a huge snake. It was about 10 feet long and Chloe was scared to death. She was crying and growling and barking. I thought I was going to have to pick up the snake and move it myself."

"DOGWOOD!" Chloe responded! "That didn't happen. Woody, tell Mom and Dad the truth."

"Maybe the snake wasn't 10 feet long," I said, knowing it was wrong to fib. Chloe rolled her eyes and Mom and Dad laughed. Once our tent was ready, our firewood was gathered, and our food was put away, our parents explained fire safety.

"Pups, campfires are fun, but they're a big responsibility. We must keep the fire small and never leave it unattended. We also must have water with us at all times in case the fire gets out of control. "

Once we understood the rules, we gathered around the fire and sang some more camp songs. I wanted to sing every verse of *John Jacob Jingleheimer Schmidt*, but my eyes were heavy.

"Tomorrow's a full day, pups. You two go to bed and Dad and I will stay up for a while to make sure the fire is completely out," Mom instructed. I knew I would be asleep as soon as my head hit the pillow. Chloe and I walked in our pup tent and I pulled back my sleeping bag. *"MO-OM!!! DA-AD!!! HELP!!!"*

Chapter 6

Already, I'd learned valuable lessons. Preparation is essential, shortcuts aren't always shorter, and rubber snakes look real! When I pulled back the cover and saw the creature, I almost fainted. Imagine my surprise when Chloe grabbed the snake, kissed it and asked if we could keep it! Score one for Chloe – joke on me! My first instinct was anger, but I realized it was a prank. I had learned one lesson long ago –to laugh at myself! Besides, I'd been the prankster before! I chuckled and wrapped the snake around my neck. After changing my pajamas, I crawled back in bed.

In what seemed like minutes, Mom called my name. "C'mon Woody. Time to eat." I stretched my body and looked outside. Mom was cooking oatmeal over our campfire. Birds were singing, squirrels were gathering breakfast, and a baby deer was lapping from a brook. My usual breakfast was a bacon sandwich in front of the TV, yet nothing compared to eating outside with my family. The scenery was more exciting than any *WOOF* game, and my food was scrumptious! My family must have felt the same because we paused to give thanks.

After cleaning our mess, we gathered our fishing gear and fishing licenses, lathered ourselves in sunscreen and journeyed

to the lake. Mom explained that we'd be fishing from the bank, but we still had to wear life preservers at all times."You know Dad, we haven't had a challenge since the backpack contest. Let's see who catches more fish." Dad agreed and Chloe and I began the friendly competition.

We cast our line and waited… and waited…

"Woody, this isn't *Pirate Pete's* where we get the fisherman's platter in three minutes," Mom whispered, sensing my frustration. "A rule in surviving is being patient, knowing the outcome will be worth the wait."

Just then, my bobber went under water, indicating a bite. "I've got one!" I shouted.

"Reel it in!" Everyone cheered. Together, Dad and I struggled to capture the gigantic creature. I was certain it was a 20-pound largemouth bass!

"Way to go, Woody! Looks like a 1 pound bluegill!"

Well, I may not have caught Baby Beluga, but it was cause for celebration!

While celebrating, a park ranger named Ranger Ralph appeared, asking for our fishing license. We introduced ourselves, showed our license, and explained the contest. "Remember the rules - you can only catch a certain number of fish – depending on the species. You can always *catch-and-release*. You can catch the fish and then throw them back in the lake." Ranger Ralph explained. "That allows you to enjoy fishing without taking the fish out of water. You can use what you catch to count toward the competition." As we caught fish, Ranger Ralph identified the species, then we released them back in the water. We learned the difference between carp, bass, and catfish. Chloe and I counted our catches. I'd caught 4 fish, 1 turtle, 2 sticks, and a smelly sock. Chloe had reeled in 3 fish, a soda can, and a shoe. I'd won!

Though Chloe had lost, she was gracious. I realized a rule in surviving was being a great sport whether I'd won or lost! Besides, we were tied. Chloe had won the packing challenge; I'd won the fishing challenge.

"Time to clean up, fisherpups," Dad said, handing us garbage bags. "Let's pick up all the trash, whether it's ours or not." We threw away the shoe, sock, soda cans, candy wrappers, fishing line, and plastic bags.

"Woody," Chloe yipped, "do you remember the documentary we watched that said plastic bags, fishing line and other trash killed wildlife?" I remembered seeing images of animals being suffocated by plastic bags and birds tangled in fishing line. "If everybody picked up their trash, the lake would never be dirty. And wildlife wouldn't die."

"Terrific point, Chloe!" Ranger Ralph said. "Think about how smooth life would be if everyone contributed." I made another note to self to do my share!

We thanked Ranger Ralph, gathered our belongings and walked toward our tent. While walking, I pulled out my harmonica. "Better put it away, son." Dad said, looking at the sky. "It'll be raining soon."

"Raining?" I asked, shoving the harmonica in my backpack.

"Yes," Dad said, "do you see the cloud in the west moving closer? There are other signs too. The crickets are louder and the tulips have closed. Being aware of nature's signs can make the difference in surviving." Just then, the sky opened, pouring buckets of water. We ran like lightening and didn't stop until we reached the tent! After drying off, I decided to play my harmonica. I opened up my backpack. Wait! Where was my instrument? Oh no, I must have dropped it...

Chapter 7

My harmonica had to be here somewhere. I had it before we arrived at the tent. It was raining cats and wiener dogs! I should have worn my raincoat, but I didn't know I would be gone so long. Oh no! I hadn't told my family I was leaving. When I realized I'd dropped my harmonica, I thought I could walk outside the tent and find it. I had meandered off in the pouring rain without telling anyone. I was in trouble – in more ways than one! I had a strong suspicion the doghouse was in my future. My goal was to locate my instrument and return to the tent. *Think, Woody, think.* If I were a harmonica, where would I be?

Our family had played so much *I Spy* lately that surely I could discover a musical instrument in the wilderness. While digging feverishly behind a row of bushes, I felt something under my paw. Could it be? YES! My beloved harmonica! I played a note. The note bubbled and gurgled. It sounded like I was playing my harmonica underwater. I tried to shake the rainwater out, but it was tough since water was pouring from the sky. Once it dried, it would be as good as new. I had to get back to the tent pronto! The rain in my eyes made it difficult to see. Where was the tent? I thought it was this way. Maybe it was back the other way. What direction was I going? If the sun set in the west, then west was??? How could I tell where

west was without the sun shining? Maybe I should go further this way. Wait - I don't rememberimg seeing that Dogwood tree before. The Dogwood tree was one tree I knew since it was my name. One thing was for sure – I was lost. I was lost, wet, cold, scared, and hungry. I remembered Mom and Dad talking to Chloe and me about what to do if we ever got lost. "If you're ever lost, find a man or woman in uniform – like a police officer - or find a store clerk wearing a nametag. Don't ever leave with a stranger and don't panic. If you're alone, stay put, stay positive, and we'll find you." Those words kept playing in my head – "stay put, stay positive, and we'll find you." It was hard to stay positive when I was terrified. At least it wasn't storming. It was just a hard rain. I was glad it wasn't lightning since I was holding a metal harmonica. Mom and Dad had taught us about storm safety – and one thing they said was never be around anything metal during a storm. I also knew being under a tree could be dangerous in case lightening struck a tree or the limbs fell. I decided to return to the bushes where I'd found my harmonica. I could sit under the bush and not be in danger of falling limbs. Maybe Ranger Ralph would show up!

It was c-c-c-cold. I wish I'd worn that raincoat. Now I knew why Mom made us dress warm when we went outside. If only I had Chloe's cell phone or weather radio. I was alone, *sniff*, shivering, scared, and starving. "Stay positive, Woody," my inner voice kept saying. I had to keep my mind off my troubles. I guess I could practice my harmonica. I played all my favorite songs – "The Ants Go Marching," "Eating Goober Peas," and the "Song that Never Ends." That one took forever! My paws were exhausted and cold from playing so long. They needed a break. It felt like they were getting numb. Maybe I would sing. I needed something happy – a song that always made me laugh, even though I didn't feel like laughing. I knew the perfect one.

Pretending I was at the Kodak Theater in Hollywood, I cleared my throat and started to sing. "On top of *puh-sketti*, all covered with cheese, I lost my poor meatball..."

You know, singing about food might not have been such a great idea. I was so hungry that I almost felt sick. I thought about eating some berries but I remember Dad telling us that we couldn't eat berries or mushrooms since they could be poisonous. I guess I would go back to singing about food.

"I lost my poor meatball, when somebody...

What was that? I listened for it again. All was silent. It must have been my stomach. I was so hungry and singing about my favorite pasta dish didn't help matters. I started singing again.

When somebody ...

Why couldn't I remember the words? This was my favorite song and I couldn't remember the words. Just then, I heard rustling in the woods. It was coming closer and closer...

Chapter 8

Where could my brother be? When he realized he'd lost his harmonica, he left the tent before we could stop him. Dad immediately went to find Woody. "Don't worry, Chloe," Dad reassured me. "I'll find your brother. You and Mom get warm clothes ready for Woody. I'm sure he's one chilly dog by now!" While Dad was gone, Mom and I gathered up towels and blankets so Woody could get dry and warm. Gathering up the towels, I saw Woody's backpack. The pupcorn, electric blanket, and art supplies were still stuffed in the bag. Even though I was sad, the backpack made me giggle. Nobody made me smile like Woody!

While we worked, Mom started singing. At the sound of her first note, my heart sank. Mom had always taught us that music could help calm the soul. Mom sang when she was happy, but she also sang when she was worried or sad. My stomach churned and my eyes burned. I'd been suffering from allergies all week, but these tears had nothing to do with dandelions or clover. Mom caught a glimpse of my face and scooped me up.

"It's okay, Chloe. Dad will find Woody. Just be positive and have faith."

"I know, Mom, but Woody is alone. I know he's starving because he talked about food all day! And he didn't have a raincoat!"

Mom wiped my tears and held me tight. "Don't worry, honey. Woody can be goofy and silly, but he's a really smart pup. He has great instincts and he has learned lots of skills since we have been camping! And his big sister has taught him a thing or two." Mom always knew how to make me smile. We returned to our chores, trying to pass the time. Finally, after almost an hour, Dad walked back in the tent. Alone.

"Bad news. I couldn't find him. I searched all around, called his name, but didn't see him." Mom and I began to sob. "Don't be scared," Dad gently said. "I'm sure he found shelter and is so protected that he couldn't hear me calling." The three of us were all thinking the same thing – Woody had been gone too long. The weather was nasty and we only had about an hour of daylight left. "I know! I'll use my cell phone and call the campground office. Maybe Ranger Ralph will be there!" I grabbed my phone while Mom retrieved the number. My paws were shaking so much it was hard to dial. It rang, and rang, and rang. Finally an answer. "Thank you for calling the *Daniel Boone Campground.* Our office is currently closed. We're open from 9 to 5 each weekday. Please leave a message after the beep." After the beep, I began to speak. "This is Chloe. My brother Woody is lost. We were hoping Ranger Ralph could help us find him." Feeling defeated, I hung up the phone.

"I think we should all go look for Woody," Mom cried. Dad suggested that he and I look for Woody while Mom stayed at the tent in case Woody returned. "But what if Chloe gets lost?" Mom argued. I assured Mom I would take my compass, map, flashlight, and even cell phone. Mom still wasn't convinced I should go. Trying to reassure her, I remembered something I had read in my camping book. "I could mark a trail!" I said. "I'll mark trees all along the way so I can find my way back in case I get confused."

"Excellent idea, Chloe!" Dad said, patting me on the head. "But how will you mark the tree?"

I giggled to myself, knowing exactly how Woody would mark the tree. "I can use the paint from Woody's Scooby Doo art set he packed." Mom and Dad looked at each other. "Brilliant!" Mom said.

We unzipped Woody's backpack and retrieved the art set. It was still sticky from the pupscicles. We decided I would mark the stump of every few trees with hot pink paint. Dad took along the bright purple paint to mark his trail. We also took high-pitched whistles in case we needed to alert each other. Dad and I decided that if we needed help, we would blow our whistle three times over and over until the other one arrived. If we found Woody, we would blow our whistle four times to signal "Hip, Hip, Hoo-ray!"

Mom made sure we were dressed warmly and had all our supplies. Before leaving, Mom, Dad, and I reviewed our plan. Mom hugged and kissed Dad and me and told us to be careful. Dad rubbed my head and told me he had complete confidence in me. With that, we left the tent and braved the elements. As I trotted away, I could hear Mom singing.

Chapter 9

Right after I left the tent, I began marking the tree stumps with pink paint. I looked behind every bush and under every rock I saw. I was so scared when I moved a rock and a snake scurried away! I hoped Woody hadn't encountered any snakes. I called Woody's name over and over, but he didn't respond. Continually marking the stumps, I tried to constantly be aware of my surroundings. I spotted a Dogwood tree and smiled. That was my brother's favorite tree! Maybe I would bring Woody back to see it after we found him. Finally, I heard something. It sounded like singing. I listened. It was singing – Woody's singing! It was the sweetest voice I'd heard! Unfortunately, I still couldn't see Woody!

I tried howling. Dogs know that howling is a form of communication – a way of saying, "Hey! I'm here," yet Woody didn't answer. So, I kept following the sound of Woody's voice until I saw him under the bushes. Once again, I howled, but Woody didn't respond. I knew I would have to go get him. But before I got to Woody, I tripped and fell in a patch of clover – the very thing I'm terribly allergic to and sneezed the biggest sneeze ever! You could have heard it all over the state!

My brother heard it too because I saw him peak his head out from behind a bush! I ran to Woody and we hugged. He was shaking like a leaf! I blew my whistle four times like Dad had

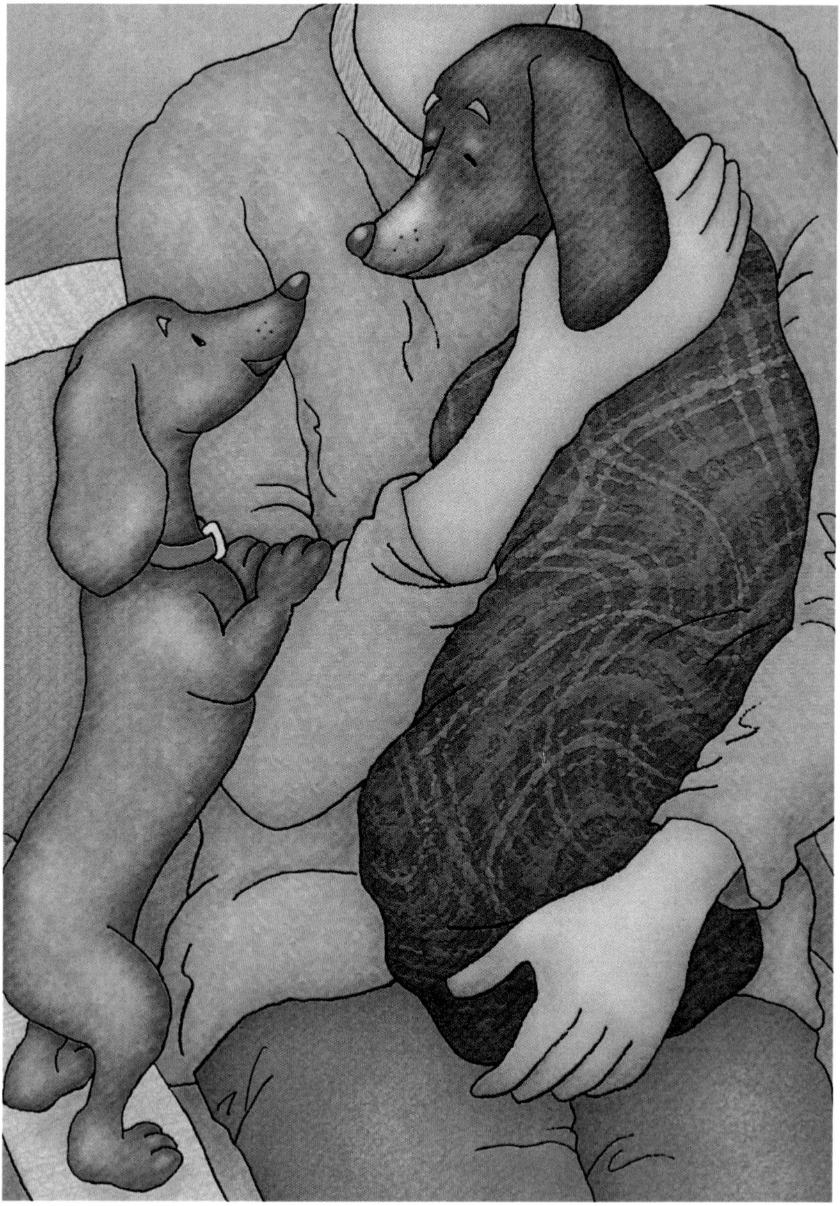

told me, and following the tree markings, I helped my brother back to our tent.

When we arrived, Woody was still trembling. I thought he was scared but Mom said he had gotten too cold and wet. Mom said that even though Woody was safe, he was in danger of hypothermia. I asked Mom what hypothermia was. "It's when people or animals get really cold and the body temperature drops below the normal level. It can be very serious – even deadly." I was worried about Woody. "Why do you think Woody has hypothermia, Mom?"

"Well, Chloe, for one, he's shivering. That's a big sign. Sure, he's shivering because he was scared, but he is really cold. He's also mumbling a bit. Sometimes people can mumble, stumble, or grumble when they are hypothermic. He was outside in the cool rain and didn't have his hat, gloves, or boots. He lost a lot of body heat through his head and paws. We have to help Woody get warm again."

I looked at my brother. His teeth were chattering and he was quivering. Mom and Dad dried Woody off and wrapped him from head to paw in warm dry blankets. Mom held Woody tight so he could feel her body heat while Dad heated some broth over the fire for my brother to drink. Mom said it was important that we warm Woody up without making him too hot since that could be just as dangerous. As Woody slowly drank the warm broth, he calmed down and his eyes brightened. It was as if we could see Woody warming up before our eyes!

After Woody started feeling better, he began to talk. At first he was still mumbling and it was hard to understand him. All we could make out was "life." Finally, as he warmed up even more, we understood what Woody was saying.

"You saved my life, Chloe! If you hadn't found me, I could

have died! How will I ever repay you for saving my life? You're a hero!"

As my brother talked, he cried a little. Mom wiped Woody's tears while Dad spoke. "Chloe is a hero, Woody, but you're a survivor!"

"I am?" Woody asked.

"Sure, Woody, you made some poor choices that could have been extremely dangerous, but you certainly were a survivor."

"How?" Woody questioned. Dad explained that once Woody knew he was lost, he sought shelter in a safe place. He also didn't continue wandering around trying to find his way. He stayed where he was. "And," Dad continued, "you were smart to play and sing the entire time. We could hear you and therefore could find you. A rule in surviving is staying calm and thinking smart when you're in a tough situation."

"Dad's right, Woody, you are a survivor!"

"Thanks Chloe, but you're still my hero! There has to be something I can do for you since you saved my life."

I didn't feel right about asking my brother to do something for me, but I could tell he wasn't going to feel better unless I agreed he could help me. Finally, I gave in. "Well, Woody, if you insist. There is one thing I would love."

"Anything, Chloe! Just say the word!"

Chapter 10

"You want me to do what?" I asked Chloe! "You heard me, Woody. I want you to take the prize money." My ears must have still been water logged. "Why would you want me to take the money, Chloe?" I asked.

"Because you are a survivor. It's hard to believe that the pup who survived alone in the rain is the same one who packed a plug-in blanket." Everyone giggled.

"But Chloe, we're tied in the challenges. You won the backpack challenge, I won the fishing challenge."

"Yes, Woody, but you survived a real situation – not a challenge."

I tried to remind Chloe that she had survived in a real situation by rescuing me, but she wasn't listening. "I'll agree with you on one point, Chloe. I have come along way!" Again, everyone giggled – and agreed. "Tell us about it, son." Dad said.

"Well, I learned that to survive in the wilderness, you have to make smart choices and be prepared. My life would have been easier if I'd packed my hat instead of pupscicles. I learned it's great to work together to accomplish a task. When Chloe and I put our heads together, we mapped our journey, escaped a snake, and were there for each other when things got sticky." Mom and Dad looked pleased, so I continued. "I learned shortcuts aren't always shorter and I learned being able to read and

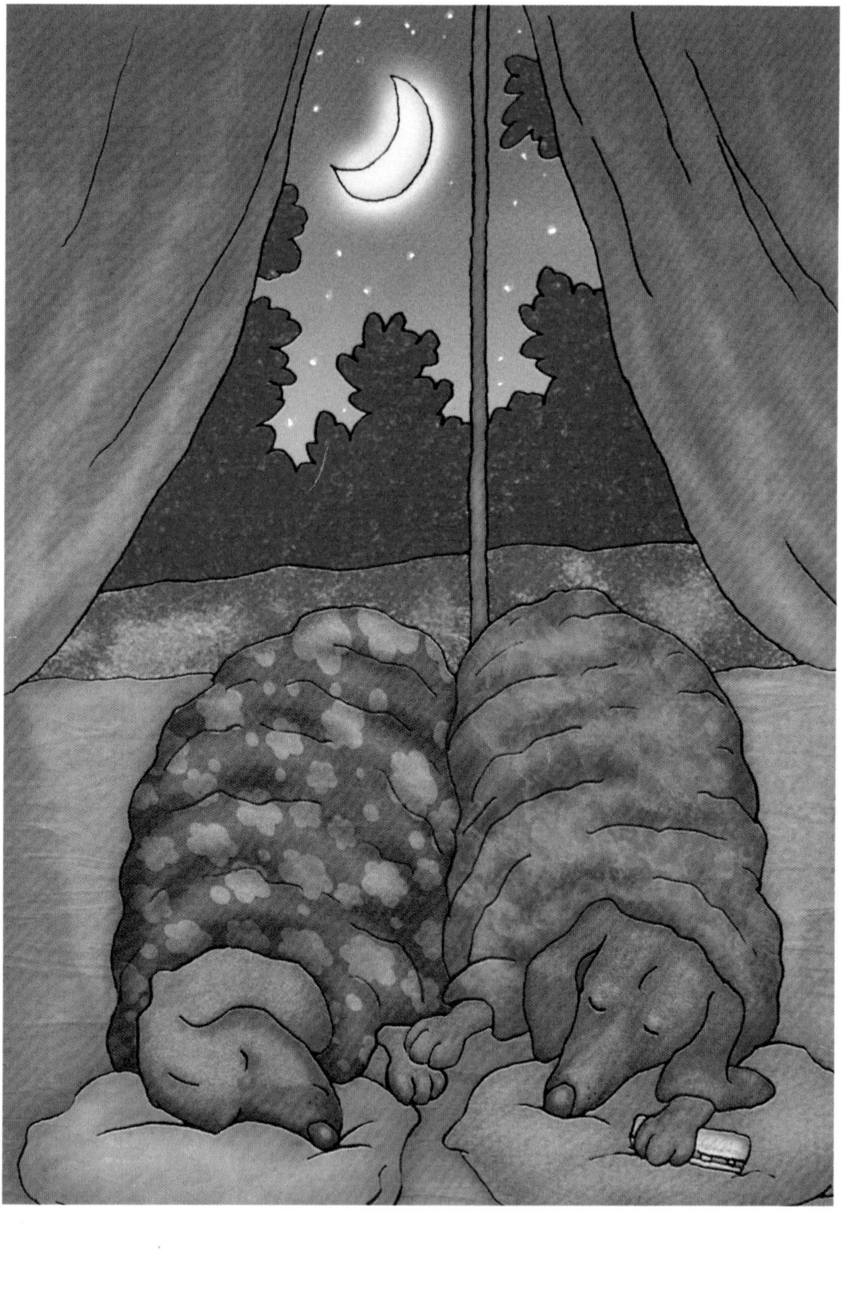

communicate is necessary in surviving."

"Anything else?" Mom asked. "I learned we must follow the rules even when nobody is watching. And if everyone does his part, then life will be smoother and happier for us all. I learned when you find yourself in a pickle, it's important to keep a cool head and stay positive. And, if you're ever in the woods alone and you don't have a cell phone or a compass, a harmonica could save your life!"

Mom, Dad, and Chloe laughed! "We should camp more often, especially now that I know how to survive at camping," I suggested. Dad agreed that we would be camping regularly, but then he said something that surprised me.

"Woody, you didn't just learn about surviving in the wilderness."

"I didn't?"

"No, you learned about surviving in real life. Think about it. All the points you listed apply to real life. Your mom and I are always talking about how important it is to be able to read, follow directions, and communicate with others. We are always talking about staying cool in tough situations and making smart choices."

Dad was right. The light bulb in my head turned on. "Now I know why Mom is always reading books to us and teaching us new words. I'm sorry, Mom. Sometimes I thought you made us follow directions because that's what Moms did. I didn't realize you were helping us be survivors." Mom gave me the best hug.

I looked at Mom and realized something else. "I also know why you won't let me spend all my time in front of the TV playing my *WOOF* game. You knew there was a great big world outside that was more exciting, colorful and challe- ing than any computer program or DVD in the world."

looked at Dad, who was holding Chloe, and said, "By doggies, I think he's got it!" Chloe crawled off Dad's knee and joined me in Mom's lap.

"That's why you have to take the prize money, Woody. You earned it!"

I thought about it for a second. "That's so generous of you, Chloe, but you know, the *WOOF* game I wanted isn't exciting anymore. I don't need the money now."

"Yes, you do!"

"I do?"

"Definitely!"

I was confused. Why did Chloe think I needed the money so badly? "I hate to argue, Chloe, but I don't want the game anymore. I want to do something for you. You rescued me in the woods – and besides, you come to my rescue all the time!"

Chloe looked exasperated. "Woody, by taking the money, you WILL be doing a big favor for the whole family."

"I will?"

"Yes," Chloe answered. "I want you to use the money for harmonica lessons!" Everyone roared with laughter. I gave Chloe a bear hug and thanked her for the generous gift. Chloe had just taught me one more thing. I wasn't the harmonica virtuoso that I thought.

"It's been a long day, pups," Dad said. "Let's get a good night sleep. We have lots of camping left before we head home in a few days." Mom tucked us in our sleeping bags, read us a story, and we said our bedtime prayers, being thankful for our safety. I snuggled up to Chloe. I took my right paw and wrapped it around Chloe's paw. In my left paw was, you guessed it, my harmonica.

Woodys Favorite Campfire Songs and Harmonica Solos

America

On Top of Spaghetti

The Bear Went Over the Mountain

John Jacob Jingleheimer Schmidt

Go Tell Aunt Rhody

Billy Boy

She'll Be Coming Round the Mountain

Woody and Chloes Favorite Travel Games

The Alphabet Game

I Spy

Name That Tune

First Aid Kit

A first aid kit is very important for everyone to have. The Red Cross recommends that all first aid kits for a family of four include the following:

- 2 absorbent compress dressings (5 x 9 inches)
- 25 adhesive bandages (assorted sizes)
- 1 adhesive cloth tape (10 yards x 1 inch)
- 5 antibiotic ointment packets (approximately 1 gram)
- 5 antiseptic wipe packets
- 2 packets of aspirin (81 mg each)
- 1 blanket (space blanket)
- 1 breathing barrier (with one-way valve)
- 1 instant cold compress
- 2 pair of nonlatex gloves (size: large)
- 2 hydrocortisone ointment packets (approximately 1 gram each)
- Scissors
- 1 roller bandage (3 inches wide)
- 1 roller bandage (4 inches wide)
- 5 sterile gauze pads (3 x 3 inches)
- 5 sterile gauze pads (4 x 4 inches)
- Oral thermometer (non-mercury - nonglass)
- 2 triangular bandages
- Tweezer
- First aid instruction booklet

Woodys World Famous Puh-Sketti Recipe

Here are the ingredients (the things you will need):

1 pound hamburger (not a hamburger with the bun, mustard, or pickles - just the meat)
1 onion, chopped (be prepared to cry)
1 6 ounce can tomato paste (not to be confused with tooth paste or glue paste)
3 small cans tomato sauce
1 tablespoon sugar
1/4 cup Parmesan cheese

Spaghetti noodles

Directions:

Make sure you have an adult who actually knows his or her way around the kitchen. A good test is whether they know the difference between a stove and an oven. If so, you are in business!

In a pan on the stove, brown hamburger and onions. Pour off all the fat. (We thought the fat looked delicious, but Mom said we couldn't eat the fat.) Add remaining ingredients to the hamburger and onions. Simmer 2-3 hours. (Simmer means to keep it hot but don't let it boil.) Serve over spaghetti noodles.

It taste great with a salad on the side, maybe a stick or two of beef jerky, and a fresh bowl of water to keep the whistle wet! Top it off with Vanilla WOOFERS and a small dish of ice cream for dessert! Talk about a meal fit for a King!

Woody and Chloes Favorite Riddles

1. How do fleas travel from place to place?

   An Itch Hiker

2. What game do cows play at parties?

   Mooooosical Chairs

3. What did the frog order from the drive-thru?

   Flies and a Croak

4. What do you get if you cross a skunk and a teddy bear?

   Winnie the Phew